MAGUS
AND
THE BLUE FAIRY

Maureen Lyall

To Rohan Brian
Agarwal
Enjoy
Maureen Lyall

AuthorHouse™
1663 Liberty Drive
Bloomington, IN 47403
www.authorhouse.com
Phone: 1-800-839-8640

Published by AuthorHouse 08/27/2012

ISBN: 978-1-4772-6562-8 (sc)
978-1-4772-6563-5 (e)

Library of Congress Control Number: 2012916058

Any people depicted in stock imagery provided by Thinkstock are models,
and such images are being used for illustrative purposes only.
Certain stock imagery © Thinkstock.

This book is printed on acid-free paper.

authorHOUSE®

To **ESHAN**

Thank you for being so much FUN!!!

Once there was a wee little man who was 3 feet tall, named Magus, who lived deep in the woods. Magus lived in his house all alone in the woods, and he did not have a friend in the world, he did not see the need to have friends. Once he tried to be friends with the neighbor boys, but they teased him and broke his fishing rod. After that incident Magus did not worry about the boys, he had no time to play with them anyway, because he spent every minute of his free time fishing.

Magus loved to fish, so every morning he would go into the yard and dig up some worms, and put them into a tin pail. Then he would walk to the lake where his boat was moored, he did this everyday.

While fishing in his boat, 'the Dragon-Fly', Magus always felt like he was flying over the water, which in the bright sunlight always glistened and sparkled like diamonds.

Since he spent every minute of his free time on the boat Magus did not see the need to have friends, he saw no one as he was on his boat early in the morning and he went home sometimes late in the night.

But things always change, Magus found that out.

One day while walking on the on the rocky road to the lake, Magus was deep in thought, and failed to see the Blue Fairy appear in front of him. The Blue Fairy was the fairy who took care of the people of the woods, and was named Blue, because she always wore blue clothes and carried a blue wand. The Blue Fairy was concerned with Magus' lack of friends and was determined that Magus should become more social.

"Hello Magus, where are you going?"

Startled out of his thoughts Magus saw the Blue Fairy and said, "Fishing." Magus did not like to talk or be with others. Needless to say, he did not want any friends, and he was always rude to people who spoke to him.

The Blue Fairy failed to understand that Magus wanted to be alone and continued to hover over him and said, "I would love to fish with you."

"I don't think you would like to fish with me Ma'am." Magus said.

Magus did not want anyone to fish with him, he liked to be alone in his boat and dream that he was flying with the seagulls in the sky. Besides talking to and being with people scared him.

"Oh please Magus let me come; I have never fished in my entire life. I want to learn", the Blue Fairy said.

"But you can't fish with me." Magus said brightening up as he got an idea. "You don't have a fishing rod."

"No problem", the Blue Fairy snapped her fingers and she held a brand new fishing rod.

When Magus saw the fishing rod, he knew he had to let her come with him, so he said. "Well come on."

At the lake, Magus helped the Blue Fairy into the boat, pushed the boat out, and showed the Blue Fairy how to use her fishing road.

Magus had always thought that fishing with someone else would be boring, but it was fun, because while fishing, the Blue Fairy told him stories about her travels to different countries. He enjoyed listening to the stories, and got over his shyness by slowly starting to tell his fishing stories to the Blue Fairy.

Time flew by and before Magus knew it, he and the Blue Fairy were tying up the 'Dragon-Fly'.

On the way home they talked about how much fun it was to fish and when they should go again.

When they reached Magus' house the Blue Fairy stayed for supper, they cooked the days catch.

The next morning Magus went out into the back yard and dug up some worms. He wished the Blue Fairy would come and fish with him today, but of course she had other things to do. On the path to the lake, he heard some voices behind him and turned around to look. It was the Blue Fairy and she had 2 boys with her.

11

Remember I told you that the Blue Fairy took care of the folks who lived in the woods; well the Blue Fairy brought the 2 boys from the city to fish with Magus because she was concerned that the city boys were missing all the fun, people have in the great outdoors.

"Hi Magus, I thought I missed you. Yesterday I had so much fun fishing with you on the lake that I thought you would like to take 2 of my friends from the city with you, today." the Blue Fairy said.

Magus did not want to take the 2 boys fishing, he did not want to run after them and miss a perfectly good day of fishing. But Magus thought, he did have fun fishing with the Blue Fairy yesterday, and he did like listening to her stories. More then anything he wanted to be friends with the Blue Fairy.

So Magus told the Blue Fairy, "Alright, I'll take the 2 boys fishing with me." But he was not looking forward to being teased by Harry and Burt.

The Blue Fairy said, "Oh good Magus, this is Harry and Burt. Boys have fun fishing with Magus. He has a cool boat named, 'the Dragon-Fly'."

Magus found that he did have fun fishing with Harry and Burt. They did not tease him like the other boys. He showed them how to dig for worms and in the boat he taught them how to fish. The two boys loved the Dragon-Fly and soon were able to sail her without Magus' help. Harry loved to climb to the top of the sail and pretend that he was flying with the birds in the sky.

While fishing Magus told Harry and Burt all the stories he knew. The two boys told Magus Stories about living in the city. Magus listened to their stories and knew that he would not like living in the city, for one thing, he would not have his boat with him, and he would not be able to fish in the city.

Remember, I told you that Magus did not like to fish with other people. Well, after that day Magus did not like to fish by himself, because he found that he had more fun fishing and sharing his adventures with friends.

In fact, Magus, Harry and Burt did become friends and had many fishing adventures together, but that is another story.

THE END

CPSIA information can be obtained
at www.ICGtesting.com
Printed in the USA
LVIC06n2053101013
356235LV00002B